W9-BQS-689

Biscuit's
Show and Share Day

by Alyssa Satin Capucilli
pictures by Mary O'Keefe Young

HarperFestival®
A Division of HarperCollinsPublishers

"Today is show and share day at school, Biscuit.
What shall I bring to show and share with my class?"
Woof, woof!

"Maybe I will bring my favorite teddy bear."
Woof, woof!

"Funny puppy!
You found your favorite blanket."
Woof!

"A seashell would be fun to show and share,
or a picture of the new baby!"
Woof, woof!

"Silly puppy!
It's not time to play ball now.
It's almost time for school."

"Now, let's see. What shall I bring?"
Woof, woof! Woof, woof!

"Oh, no, Biscuit.
How did you get that box of biscuits?"
Woof!

Beep! Beep!
"There's the school bus, Biscuit.
It's time for school!"
Woof, woof!

"Wait, Biscuit. Come back!
Where are you going with my backpack?"
Woof, woof!

"Oh, Biscuit.
You want to go to school today.
You want to be my show and share!"
Woof, woof!

"I can hardly wait for everyone to meet you, Biscuit.
Come along, sweet puppy!
There's my teacher."
Woof, woof!

"Welcome to school, Biscuit.
This is going to be the most special
show and share day of all!"
Woof, woof!

Which Way?
Help Biscuit find his way to school!

To see the answer, turn to the last page.

Snack Time

It's time for a treat!

What does Biscuit like to eat?

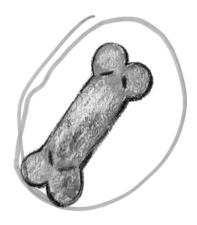

To see the answer, turn to the last page.

Mixed-Up Words

These words are all mixed-up! Can you fix them?
Here's a hint—they're all in the story!

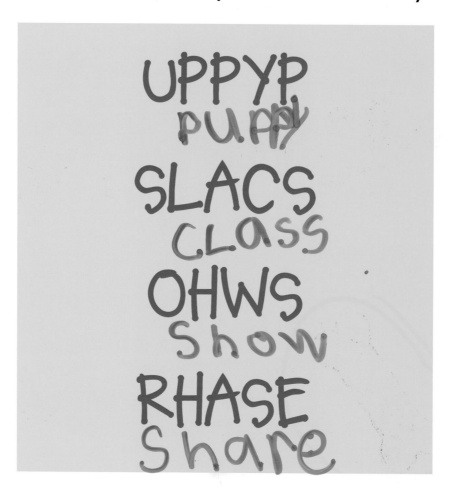

UPPYP
PUPPY

SLACS
CLASS

OHWS
Show

RHASE
Share

To see the answers, turn to the last page.

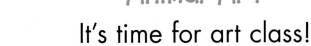

Animal Art

It's time for art class!

Can you draw your favorite animal?

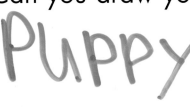

PuPPy

Find the Difference

Look closely at these pictures.
Which one is different?

To see the answer, turn to the last page.

Word Search

Can you find these words in the puzzle below?
Circle each one you find.
Be sure to look across and down!

SCHOOL   BISCUIT   BACKPACK   TEACHER   WOOF

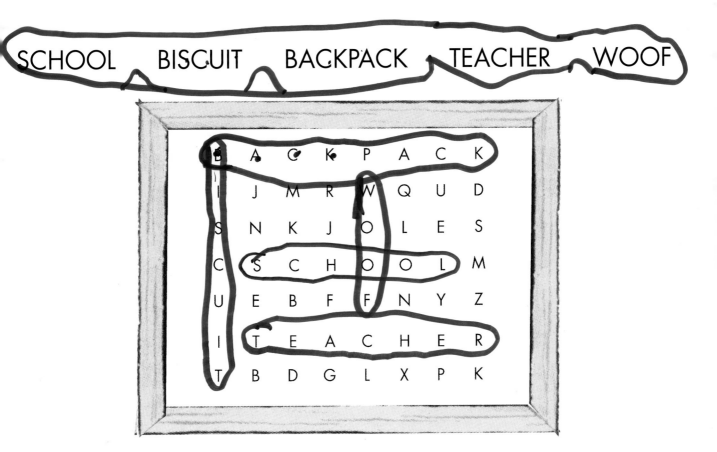

To see the answers, turn to the last page.

Answer Key

Which Way?

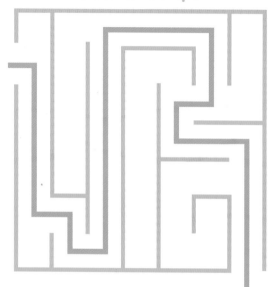

Mixed-Up Words

Puppy, Class, Show, Share

Find the Difference

Snack Time

Word Search

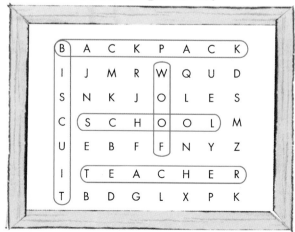